Planet of Stones

David R. Beshears

Based on the screenplay
"Planet of Stones"

Greybeard Publishing
Washington State

Greybeard Publishing
P.O. Box 480
McCleary, WA 98557-0480

ISBN 978-0-9987535-0-8

Planet of Stones

One

The gently sloping mountains were covered in a forest of tall trees, mostly fir and the occasional alder. The forest floor was a thick mulch of fir needles and twigs and a scattered sparse undergrowth of fern, was shadowed by the high canopy above.

A lone man followed a well-traveled trail, moving in and out of the shadows as he walked a casual, easy pace. He held a tall, wooden hiking staff in hand, wore a light backpack on his back. The figure was little more than a silhouette set against the shadows, with occasional rays of sunlight brushing across his frame as he passed through shimmering, mote-filled shafts of light. The world was quiet. Even the man's footfalls were muffled as he walked the mulch-covered path.

He followed the trail into a forest clearing, walked past a rustic root cellar door that was set into the ground and continued on toward the outpost; a wall set into the side of a brush-covered mound.

Lieutenant Connelly was in his mid-thirties. He had a medium build, was clean shaven, and dressed in rugged, well-made clothes and boots. The brown hair pushing out from under his cap had grown longer than was standard for a military officer.

He leaned his staff against the wall beside the door, pressed the palm of one hand against the ident panel set next to the door. There was a hollow click sound. He lifted the latch and slid it aside, opened the door.

The station's main cabin was twelve feet wide by sixteen feet deep. The two long walls were lined with shelves, workbenches and cabinets. There was a narrow cot at the far end, a small table in the middle of the room.

Connelly slipped out of his gear, stowed the pack and his utility belt under a counter. He took A-I Box out of his pocket and set it on the workbench. The high-tech artificial intelligence device was a thin, palm-sized box of molded plastic.

He continued then across the room and stepped through a narrow door threshold.

The back room was small, with one counter and one chair. Connelly sat down and scooted forward. He picked up the headset mic and put it on, reached out to an equipment panel that was against the wall, pushed one of a row of buttons, tapped at the headset and began recording.

"Outpost Six, Connelly, log entry 433," he started. "I followed Alpha Tribe Three into the West Gorge for six days. Somewhat surprising, really. Of all the tribes, this group has been the least nomadic to now, the least likely to drift so far from home. From what I could tell, they weren't hunting, weren't foraging. They seemed to be... exploring." Connelly shook his head. "I don't know... they could have been hunting I suppose, but if they were, it wasn't for food. They were... searching."

Connelly thought on his next words for a few moments.

"Reaching the head of the gorge, they went up the hillside, over the ridge, and started back the other way. No reason that I could see. Anyway, I lost them for a time. I found their trail again, followed it back; didn't see them again until I was nearly back to the Valley. At that point, I of course steered clear, mainly to avoid having the observer observed; worked my way back."

He hesitated then, managed a playful smirk.

"I'm afraid I hurt Box. Said it before, say it again. He's not as shockproof as we were led on."

Connelly shifted position, leaned forward and held his hand on the panel. "I'll try and fix him up tomorrow. Hope he isn't too pissed." He hesitated. "Report ends."

He deactivated the recorder, pulled the headset off, tossed it onto the counter.

Connelly was sitting at his small table, absently eating from a bowl. It was late, the room quiet. He stared ahead at nothing in particular as he ate in silence.

When he finished his meal, he slid back from the table, stood and took the several short steps over to the basin. He took his time washing the bowl and spoon. He set them into the tray to dry.

One overhead light was turned on, set very low. Connelly was asleep in his cot.

The sound of a soft alert delicately pushed at the quiet. The overhead light blinked half a dozen times, paused, then blinked again.

Connelly rolled sluggishly onto his side and sat up. He stood up and slowly stepped over to the communication station and dropped into the chair. He reached out and flipped a switch.

"Connelly here," he stated.

The sound of the Major's voice came through the small speaker. It was a steady, smooth voice.

"Lieutenant. Apologies for contacting you off schedule."

"Not a problem, sir." He managed to sound sincere. "Good to hear your voice."

"That's what they all say, Lieutenant."

"Next time, I'll try to come up with something a little more original, sir."

There was a moment's hesitation, long enough for Connelly to look up at the radio.

"I'm afraid there won't be a next time," said the Major. "We are returning all personnel to Point Zero. All six Monitors are recalled to Central."

"Sir? I have eight months on my—"

"Embarkation in four days, seven hours," Major stated firmly, cutting him off.

Connelly again stared at the radio.

"Yes, sir. May I ask why?"

"No, Lieutenant."

There was a long pause in the exchange, the Major seemingly waiting for Connelly to come to terms with the new orders, Connelly struggling to take it all in.

"Very well, sir," Connelly stated at last.

"I'll see you in four days."

"Yes, sir. Connelly out." Connelly frowned as he reached out and flipped the switch, turning off the radio. He leaned back in his chair, looked uncertainly at the communication station.

He mumbled then to himself.

"That do be most curious."

Connelly sat at his workbench, working on the AI device in front of him. The back was off the case; he inserted a small tool and adjusted one of the connections.

He had been at it for about an hour, since finishing an early breakfast. He hadn't gotten much sleep after the Major's call and had finally risen early.

He took a drink from his coffee, absently set the cup back on the counter and returned to his work. After a few more adjustments, he closed the back panel and turned the device over. He used the tool to activate the device.

"Hey, Box. You in there?"

"Yes I am, Lieutenant Connelly," said Box. The voice was clear, the tone smooth and very human. "It is good to be back."

"Great." Connelly picked up his coffee cup, leaned back in his chair and took another drink.

"We are back at the outpost," stated Box.

"That's right," said Connelly. "Can you run a self-diagnostic?"

"Already done. I am fine."

"Glad to hear it." He took another sip of his coffee, managed a grin. "Sorry about the accident."

"Ah. I was wondering what happened." There was a moment's hesitation. "Nothing permanent, it would seem."

"Good." Connelly pushed back from the workbench, stood up and began putting away the tools. "It looks like we're taking another trip, Box. We're leaving for Central this morning."

"Lieutenant. We are not scheduled to return to Central for two hundred forty seven days."

"Yeah, well, change happens. Something's come up."

"Of course. I understand," said Box. "What might that something be?"

"We are returning to Point Zero. So I have been informed."

"Returning to Point Zero..."

"That's right." Connelly put the tool kit into the drawer. "And no... I haven't a clue."

Connelly climbed out of the root cellar, a canvas bag in hand. He closed the door and walked back to the outpost door. Streaks of sunlight speared through the forest of tree trunks and reached across the clearing. The world was eerily quiet, with only the faint sound of dewdrops falling from the vegetation.

Back inside, Connelly set the bag on the workbench beside the backpack and began transferring items from the bag to backpack, mostly bags of berries and assorted roots that he collected in his wanderings.

Box was on the workbench beside Connelly's gear.

"The journey to Central will need to be taken with caution," he said.

"I'll do what I can, Box. Can't do anymore than that."

"You will have only your walking staff for defense," said Box.

"As always, Box. Rules be rules." He continued packing. "What's the problem?"

"I am uncomfortable with this unexpected change in your calendar, and the unplanned, unscheduled journey to Central."

"Yeah, well, such is life." Connelly looked about the room, looking for something, for anything.

There was nothing else. He didn't have much.

"I guess that's it, then." He looked from his surroundings to the backpack. "Not much for two years of your life."

Box knew what was important...

"Have communications been secured?"

"Yes, Box."

Box hesitated, as if the A-I was lost in thought, spoke up then, almost warily.

"As I was offline when we returned to the outpost, and as you may not survive the next four days, I am obligated to ask... have your most recent observations been entered into the data crystal?"

"Have I ever not?"

"And yet I must ask."

"Yes, Box. Observations of our most recent outing have been entered. The time capsule is current."

There was yet another hesitation from Box.

"Thank you, Lieutenant Connelly."

"You're welcome, Box." Connelly closed his backpack and fastened the straps. He took a final look around the room. It had been his home for almost two years. He wondered if he would ever see it again.

Two

Connelly stepped out of the outpost. He wore his standard hiking gear of heavy shirt and pants, cap, hiking boots, utility belt and backpack. He latched the door, took his staff in hand and walked away from the station.

It was midmorning. The forest was still. Connelly worked his way up over the nearby ridge and followed the winding trail downslope on the other side. As he continued working his way down the mountain, the surrounding forest floor grew sparser. The day grew brighter as the sun rose higher and the canopy overhead thinned.

He came onto a wide path that followed the base of the next hill, this one lower and broader than the mountainside he had just descended. He followed the trail for another half hour before turning upslope and taking the hill. There were few trees now, much more brush and bramble.

Beyond this hill was another, and beyond that a third. Connelly moved out onto a rocky outcropping that looked out onto a flat plain beyond. He took it in for a few moments before stepping over to a rock that formed a natural bench. He leaned his staff against the bench and slid the backpack off his shoulder and set it on the bench. He brought out a pair of binoculars and walked again to the edge of the vista point.

He brought the binoculars up to his eyes.

The plain stretched away to the horizon. There were clusters of deciduous trees, shrubs, and spans of meadow. A river ran down the center of the plain. Green, tree-covered hills rose on either side.

Connelly lowered the binoculars, but continued to study the view with the naked eye for a long time.

Starting out again, it took him most of the afternoon to reach the plain below. He then continued north until evening, stopping for the night in a small clearing surrounded by thick brush. Far to the south, a low mountain range shadowed the horizon; his mountains.

He built a campfire in the center of the clearing, and when it was ready placed a small cooking pot above the forming coals. While his evening meal heated, he set about placing a series of small monitoring devices around the perimeter of the clearing. Kneeling then beside the last device, he pressed a small panel on the side of the sensor box.

"That's it, Box," he said.

The Box device was resting atop the backpack near the center of the clearing.

"I'm reading all four sensors, Lieutenant," he said.

Connelly stood. He looked outward, over the low brush, out across the open plain to the distant mountain range.

"Two years in the mountains," he said. "Gotta tell ya' Box, I've never much liked it out here in the open."

"We have been here on a number of previous occasions, Lieutenant." Box's words were pointed then. "All were *scheduled* excursions."

"Yeah, I get that," Connelly said, a thin smile. The smile faded and he looked up at the sky. "I need trees."

Box said nothing to that. He had heard it before.

Connelly turned back to the campfire. Dinner was just about ready.

The night sky was black. Thick, dark clouds hid the stars. Connelly lay asleep beside the campfire, which was now only dully shimmering coals, the faint light pushing a bluish glow over Connelly's face.

A soft sequence of beeping sounds, barely audible, just enough to reach the outer edges of the clearing and no further.

Connelly's eyes opened. He spoke quietly, not yet moving.

"What do we have, Box?"

"There is movement several hundred yards to the north."

"Wildlife?"

"Likely not. Six life forms."

Connelly sat up slowly, then just as slowly got to his feet. He worked his way into the brush, a dozen paces from clearing. He knelt behind a bramble of branches and vines, reached forward and pushed aside the vegetation.

A hundred yards further on, there were six figures in silhouette. They were traveling in a line moving from left to right, barely distinguishable in the night, little more than shadows. But he could see they were humanoid; the tallest stood about five foot tall, the others a bit shorter.

They moved quietly, walking smoothly, steadily.

Connelly watched the tribe of Alphas until they were out of sight. He slid back then, stood and backed away, turned and started back.

Returning to the campsite, Connelly settled back into his bedding. He got comfortable and eventually closed his eyes.

"Alphas," he said matter-of-factly.

"You are certain..."

"Pretty much."

"That would place them well outside their traditional habitat," said Box. "And they are traveling at night."

"Mmm hmm."

The world returned to its late-night peace and quiet.

Connelly's eyes slowly opened. He listened to the night.

All was still.

Connelly squatted atop a grassy hilltop, binoculars in hand, looked down into the narrow valley below. A thread of a river ran the floor, deciduous trees growing along the banks. The valley walls on either side were blanketed in evergreen.

A tribe of several dozen Alphas was working its way along the river.

Humanoid, four to five feet tall, husky, with thick arms and legs; medium complexion, skin bare with mottles of dark hair. They walked fully upright, dressed in primitive clothing with no care as to aesthetics. Their feet were well protected in simple leather covering.

Connelly slid back and slipped below the ridge on the back side of the hilltop. He sat beside his backpack and his staff.

He pulled Box from his pocket and set it on his backpack. He spoke without looking at the device.

"Alpha Valley is no longer an option," he said.

"Alpha Valley is the route to Central," said Box.

"Yeah, well, it's full of Alphas."

"They most certainly should be avoided. We must not interfere with their natural course."

"I understand that," said Connelly. There was a hint of agitation. "That and the fact that the can tear my arm off and beat me with it."

"They have shown no such inclination, Lieutenant. They are in fact for the most part non-violent."

Connelly eyed Box, growing increasingly annoyed.

"Yeah, well, when they get annoyed, ya' never know. All right?"

Box decided it best to let that go.

"As Alpha Valley is home to all of the Alpha tribes, their presence was to be expected. You will proceed with caution, Mr. Connelly."

"I shall not, Box."

"Alpha Valley is the route to Central."

"Not the only route," said Connelly. He rested his elbows on his knees. "I can go through the Black Forest."

"No you cannot," said Box. "Black Forest is not an option."

"The Alphas don't look like they're going far, and I'm on a tight schedule here. So you give me another option."

Box was silent, the device sitting on the backpack.

"Right," said Connelly. He shifted about and readied to stand up. "Black Forest it is, then."

Three

Connelly started across a large, wide field of tall grass and wildflowers. The sun was warm. A slight breeze wafted pungent aromas as his feet and legs pushed through the meadow.

Ahead was a great wall of trees that stood two hundred feet high and loomed over the terrain. Connelly continued across the meadow and approached the wall. He entered the trees.

The Black Forest was a world of shadowy dark gray, with occasional streaks of fuzzy light. Massive trees were spaced widely apart; giant ferns; an open, mulchy floor. Connelly was dwarfed by his surroundings. The narrow beam of his flashlight pierced the permanent twilight.

An hour into the world of deep, heavy, ominous silence, Connelly came upon a small brook. He slipped out of his backpack, removed a water bottle from a side pocket. He knelt and filled the bottle from the brook. He dropped purification tablets into the bottle, swirled the bottle, and took a swig.

He returned the bottle to the side pocket, looked up and away from the brook. A growling animal sound reached him from the shadows.

Connelly stood still, only his eyes moving, scanning the dark beyond the nearest trees.

Only silence now...

He slipped back into his gear. One more look at the shadows and then he stepped across the brook and continued on. He kept a casual steady pace. Following him... movement in the shadows behind the trees and brush. Glimpses of silhouettes moving parallel to Connelly. One at first, then three, then half a dozen, then more.

Barely three feet tall, they were nothing more than shadows within the shadows. They drew no nearer, seemed to be content to follow and observe.

Half an hour after leaving the brook, Connelly noticed a dozen or more faint lights ahead in the distance, some near ground level, some hanging high above the forest floor. As he approached, it was clear that they were artificial. Another minute then and he came into a large forest clearing. Lantern-like globes were hung in the surrounding treetops, giving the clearing a fuzzy glow.

There were a dozen wooden platforms scattered about the open space, each two to three feet high, surrounding a larger altar-like structure in the very center. The altar appeared to be a collection of several platforms that had been stacked precariously together. Each individual section was decorated with assorted living plants.

Eight small creatures moved from the perimeter shadows into the clearing. And then another four. And then another...

"Great," Connelly mumbled to himself. "Littles."

The Littles were three feet tall, fine featured. They had large dark eyes, clear and shining with intelligence, small nose and full mouth. Wispy hair fell past their shoulders and drifted as they moved.

Their garments were simple, well-crafted wraps that were tied at the waist, decorated with unique geometric patterns. They all wore soft foot coverings that reached above the ankles and were tied with leather straps.

Connelly stepped cautiously into the heart of the clearing. He stopped near the altar, turned slowly about as he warily watched the Little creatures close in, forming a circle that tightened about him.

He calmly shifted his staff into attack position, a warning more than a threat.

The circle of Littles stopped ten feet from Connelly. One tilted its head slightly as it studied the staff. It spoke side-glance to the others in the language of the Littles, its tone smooth and soft.

"Pen-tah, toh theh la mah the," it said.

One of the others tilted its head then, looked at Connelly as it responded to the first creature.

"Theh la mohn deh noh," it said.

The first speaker thought on that for a moment, turned its attention again to Connelly. It stared pointedly, mouth pursed. With that, several of the Little creatures started forward again, slowly closing in.

Connelly swung his staff in a level arc, which created a soft whoosh sound. The end of the staff brushed at several of the Littles and they all stopped, took a single step back. None looked to be particularly frightened; rather they appeared to be uncertain, maybe even a bit perplexed.

"Come on, fellas," said Connelly. "No reason for it to go this way. Just what seems to be the issue?"

One of the Littles calmly chattered a handful of unintelligible words and then fell silent.

"Really?" asked Connelly, albeit rather sarcastically. "Is that all?"

Two of the Littles moved incautiously. Connelly brought the staff about and jabbed it forward end first, popped one of the Littles in the chest. It stumbled back as Connelly attempted the same with the second Little. This one, however, was already stepping back and easily avoided Connelly's attack.

A moment later eight of the creatures rushed in together.

Connelly swung the staff about and jabbed it at the Littles again and again, knocking back several, forcing others to adjust tactics.

"Come on, guys."

Connelly was overwhelmed within moments, and was quickly brought to the ground. He struggled to push them off, managed to roll over onto his knees. The creatures grabbed at his arms, at his backpack, his shirt, his hair. He scrambled forward, struggled from his knees up to his feet, one of the Littles continuing to cling to Connelly's backpack. Connelly freed himself of the creature and stumbled out of the clearing at a run, somehow still hanging onto his staff.

Again in the permanent twilight of the forest floor, he moved at a quick, easy jog through the shadows. Glancing back over his shoulder, he could see the shadows within shadows... the small creatures pacing him.

Connelly sat on the trunk of a fallen tree, his open backpack beside him, along with his water bottle and a first aid kit. His shirt was open, bruises were visible, already forming on his torso amidst a number of cuts and scratches.

He spoke as he applied first aid to his wounds.

"I don't get it, Box. I've never gotten it. What do they want?"

"You, Lieutenant Connelly."

"Yeah, that's not telling me anything."

"The Littles have wanted to capture a Monitor. You have been a target since the day your presence was made known to them."

Connelly grimaced as he continued to treat the cuts and scratches.

"That doesn't give me the why."

"They clearly want you alive," Box stated. "Perhaps they seek information."

"All they gotta do is ask, my friend." Connelly picked up his water bottle and took a long drink. He lowered the bottle slowly then, stopped movement, looked coolly ahead of him.

There was a single Little standing just inside the clearing, directly ahead of Connelly.

They stared at one another, both silent for several seconds until Connelly finally spoke calmly to Box.

"Company," he said.

Box did not respond.

The Little continued to study Connelly from a distance.

Connelly slowly stood and began putting his gear together, glancing from the creature to his backpack, again to the creature. Closing his backpack, he looked across the clearing a final time.

The Little was gone. Connelly was alone.

"Okay," he said. "I wonder what that was about."

"Yes?" asked Box.

"One Little. Gone now."

"Perhaps it is time to move on, Lieutenant Connelly."

"A keen observation, Box." Connelly lifted his backpack. "We're done here."

Four

He was an insignificant figure crossing the forest floor, a drifting shadow amongst great trees and giant ferns, the beam of his flashlight stabbing at the dark out ahead of him. In the distance then, bits of gray and silver were sprinkled against the backdrop of many shades of black.

Connelly approached the edge of the forest, stepped out finally from the dark wall of trees and into a meadow of grass and wildflowers. Moving into the field, he had to shield his eyes against the bright sky, a startling contrast to the time spent in the permanent night of the Black Forest.

Reaching the far side of the meadow, he worked his way into and through high, thick brush and eventually found a wide, distinct trail leading up the valley.

"Here we go," he said, stumbling out onto the path. "Easy, here on out."

"I did advise against going into the Black Forest, Lieutenant," said Box. Connelly had buttoned the A-I device securely in his breast pocket.

"Yes you did. How very wise you are."

"And we are once again in Alpha Valley."

"Yes we are." Connelly was walking briskly up the trail. "But that was a given. I always intended to return to the valley. We have to. But now we are on the other side of the Alphas."

"We are past but the one tribe, Lieutenant."

"We came out of the forest well up the valley," Connelly said defensively. "We may be past five tribes; six tribes."

"There are only four Alpha tribes." A calm, matter-of-fact statement.

"I know that." Connelly continued up the well-traveled trail, glancing warily from side to side and into the brush. "Four tribes. So we're good."

He worked his way up the valley until evening, when he set up camp in a small open area. He decided against a campfire, even a small one, and ate cold rations. The proximity sensors were silent throughout the night, but he slept restlessly and started out again well before dawn the next morning.

He walked without a break for several hours, when he stopped briefly where the trail crossed a small brook. He refilled his water bottle and dropped in the purification tablet. He took a swig, refilled the bottle and slipped it back into the side pocket.

He had only just started out again, stepping across the brook and traveling a dozen yards, when he slowed his pace, hesitating, then stopping.

The brush on either side of the trail was thick with branches, leaves and vines, the vegetation towering three feet above him. The trail itself was six feet wide and looked to be well-traveled.

Connelly whispered to Box. "I don't think we're alone."

Looking about, he didn't see anything. But he was positive. He had heard something. Something or someone was near.

There...

He heard it again.

He pushed his way into the brush beside the trail, squatted down, pulled the brush back into place and hid from view. Moments later, the sound of movement up the trail was unmistakable.

An Alpha approached. It was following the trail and coming toward Connelly's position. Another was walking behind him, and another; a line of them.

The first passed Connelly's hiding place, followed by the second.

The third Alpha slowed, stopped near Connelly's position. It lifted his head and sniffed at the air.

The next Alpha in line shoved it from behind, grunting in irritation, urging it to continue forward.

The sniffing Alpha grunted angrily over its shoulder. It sniffed again, gave another low grunt. Its companion groused impatiently until the sniffing Alpha started forward again, the rest of the line following after.

The last of the Alphas passed Connelly and disappeared around the bend. The trail grew silent; empty and still. Another twenty seconds passed before Connelly came out of hiding, the vines and branches clinging to him. He worked his way free, looked back on the trail behind him, the way he had come, the way the Alphas had gone.

"And that do be one of those four tribes you mentioned."

"So it would seem," said Box.

"On our way then," said Connelly, turning ahead and starting forward again. "Not much further."

It was actually another four hours, not counting a brief break for lunch, before Connelly stepped from the trail and onto an open expanse several hundred yards in diameter. At the heart of the clearing stood a gray, four-sided concrete obelisk; ten feet high, eight feet wide on a side. A dozen paces to the left of the obelisk was a smooth, bench-like rock.

Connelly approached the obelisk. A steel door was set into the face. Beside the door was a small metal panel, eight inches square. Holding his staff in one hand, Connelly placed his free hand flat on the panel. The panel glowed for a moment, then faded again to gray.

A computer voice emanated from a tiny speaker set above the panel.

"Recognize Monitor Six. Connelly, Lieutenant." A moment's pause and then, "Access granted."

The door slid aside. Within the access shaft was a metal ladder leading down.

Connelly left his staff leaning on the wall beside the opening and stepped inside, onto the rungs of the ladder. The door closed as he started down.

Five

The Central Control Room was dark. The only sound was a faint background hum.

Several ceiling light panels flickered to life.

The open room was twenty feet on a side, with an island counter in the center. The smooth, glossy floor shimmered with the reflection of the overhead lighting. One wall was lined with glass cabinets, two other walls had openings leading to wide hallways.

A door panel in the fourth wall slid open.

Connelly stepped through the opening and into the room. He looked about as he shifted out of his backpack and let it slide down his arm. He set it on the floor, absently leaning it against the wall beside the slowly closing access shaft door.

He called softly into the room. "Hello hello..."

There was no response. Apparently he was alone.

He moved to the counter island. He looked along the counter surface, took two steps to his left. He tapped at the surface, waited while a section of the glass surface came to life, the light reflecting up onto his face.

He brushed his fingertips across the surface, read what displayed on the screen, tapped again.

He frowned as he read.

"Hey, Box?"

"Yes, Lieutenant?"

"Are you getting anything from Central?"

"I am not."

Connelly mumbled *hmmm* under his breath and continued working the console.

"I can't access the logs," he stated. "And there's nothing from communications." He sighed loudly and deactivated the workstation. "It looks like nobody's home."

The Major's voice then came from a hidden speaker set in the ceiling. "Lieutenant Connelly. Welcome to Central."

Connelly glanced uncertainly up and to one side.

"Major? So, there you are." He looked to the other side. "Where is that, exactly?"

"I trust your journey from Outpost Six was uneventful."

"Not really, no." Connelly continued to speak into the air, one direction and then another. "But all's well that ends well, so I understand. I'm here."

"Very good," said the Major. "I am so glad."

Connelly took a step away from the counter, looked again about the room, then questioning toward the ceiling.

Something isn't right...

"And where might you be, Sir?" he asked warily.

"I am here, Lieutenant Connelly. In Central. With you."

"Is that so?" he asked. "And the other Monitors?"

"Not to worry, Lieutenant. All will be well."

"Right," hesitantly. "Next stop, Point Zero?"

"Soon enough, Lieutenant. A minor delay, at most."

"Right." Connelly took another hesitant step from the counter island. "Hey, Box?"

"Yes, Lieutenant?"

"Did you know about this?"

"Lieutenant?"

"The Major, Box. What happened to the Major?"

"I don't understand."

Major interrupted, speaking up again.

"Lieutenant Connelly. I can assure you. I am Major Broderick."

"Eh, I'm thinking not," said Connelly matter-of-factly. "You have the Major's voice. You may well have his knowledge. But I know the Major. He has two arms, two legs and an overly large nose."

"Lieutenant?" questioned Box.

"Box, you and I have spent the last twenty eight months together in rather close quarters. I know an A-I when I'm talking to one."

"I see," said Box after a long pause.

Connelly had the odd feeling that Box was taking the time to think what this might mean.

"Did you know about this?" he asked.

"I have had no interaction with Central," stated Box. "I have been with you."

Connelly gave a slight smirk as he moved over to his backpack. He picked it up, started casually toward one of the hallways.

"Right," he said as he crossed the room. "A definite non-answer if I've ever heard one. You my friend are more human every day."

"I can assure you—"

"Uh, huh. You too, eh?" Connelly walked unhurriedly down the wide hallway, bright with white walls and a glossy floor. Light panels were set into the ceiling. He peeked curiously into one room after another as he walked, never stopping for more than a few moments. He spoke in a calm, conversational tone. "So, Major... what happened to the Major?"

"I am the—"

"Yeah, yeah..." Connelly cut him off. "What happened to the Major I stood face-to-face with two years ago? The one I shook hands with the last time I was here?"

He stepped through a doorway and into a small sleep quarters. There was a bunk, small desk and chair, with a dresser set into one wall. He tossed his backpack onto the bunk. Taking hold of the back of the chair and casually turning it around, he straddled the seat and rested his arms on the chair back.

"All right, Major," he said. "Talk to me."

"Of course, Lieutenant." The voice of the Major came through a speaker set high in the wall beside the doorway. "What would you like to talk about?"

"To start... where are the other Monitors? When are we returning to Point Zero?"

There was a long moment of silence.

"Major?" Connelly prompted.

"Yes," said Major. "Those are questions that are difficult to answer with any precision, Lieutenant."

"Try."

When Major again delayed answering, Connelly took the conversation into a slightly different direction.

"Major? Major, why did you call me back?"

There were several more moments of silence. This time Connell waited patiently for Major to respond."

"Lieutenant Connelly," Major said at last. "I would ask that you do something for me."

"So? Ask."

"I... I need you to find me. I need you to find the Major."

"Excuse me?"

"I need you to find the Major with whom you... *shook hands.*"

Connelly frowned thoughtfully, hesitated. He stood slowly then, turned the chair about and straightened it, all while he continued to wear the studied expression on his face.

"Box?" he prompted.

"I knew nothing of this, Lieutenant."

"Sure," sighed Connelly. He spoke then again to Major. "And where might I find you? Him? Whatever?"

"I believe you should first seek out the circle of stones."

Connelly stood at the island counter in Central Control, worked quietly at one of the computer consoles set into the counter surface. He had been at it for ten minutes or more, moving through one file after another.

He stopped briefly then, hesitated. He curled his brow as he studied the latest text splashing across the screen.

"This... this can't be right," he grumbled softly.

"Lieutenant?" asked Box.

"If I'm reading this right..." the words trailed off, then back. "It can't be right."

"Sir?"

"Mission records."

"Yes?"

"The Monitors. The six Monitors." The words on the screen could mean only one thing. "I am alone."

"I don't understand," said Box. "Sir, there are six of you. As you have just noted."

"Six of us, yes."

The room went quiet. There was only the now familiar background white noise of Central's environmental systems.

"Lieutenant?" urged Box.

"Six of us," Connelly sighed. "But... we're in six different times. 1,000 years apart. We have all been observing this world, this same landscape, but in different eras." He put on a dark, thoughtful frown. He looked side-glance up at the ceiling.

"Major? Major, is this true?"

There is only silence from the A-I Major.

"Talk to me," ordered Connelly. "Is this true? Am I alone?"

A few more moments of silence, and then...

"You are the most contemporary of the Monitors, Lieutenant Connelly. You are stationed 95,000 years from Point Zero, with the other Monitors stationed 1,000 years apart going back to approximately 100,000 years from Point Zero."

"No. That's not right. We were all set down 100,000 years from Point Zero." Connelly looked back to the screen inset into the counter, shaking his head uncertainly. "Together. Together."

"You left Point Zero together, Lieutenant."

"But..." Realization slowed dawned. He placed his hands palm down on the counter.

Box spoke up again. "That wasn't the mission."

"The mission changed," said Connelly. He looked up from the counter. "The mission changed?"

"The mission changed," stated Major.

"Right. How could it have changed between the time we left Point Zero and Arrival?"

"I do not know, Lieutenant Connelly. I am sorry."

"How can you not—" Connelly was growing increasingly frustrated. None of this was making any sense. "And you? Where did you come from?"

"I am the Major."

"Yeah, yeah, I get that. How did you come to be?"

"I do not know."

Connelly leaned heavily on the counter, mumbled the Major's words back at him. "I do not know, I do not know." He began absently tapping his fingertips on the glass surface. "I am really, really not smiling here."

"I understand," said the Major.

"That's great," grumbled Connelly. "You understand. That's just, you know, great."

"Lieutenant," Box interrupted. "We have the location of the circle of stones. Perhaps we can—"

"Uh, huh," groused Connelly. "Not smiling here."

Central's small mess had three round tables evenly spaced in the middle of the room. There was a counter set along one wall with a food warmer and water dispenser. Several cabinets and another counter were set against another wall.

It was late. Connelly was sitting at one of the tables. There was a water glass and a bowl on the table in front of him. He ate his meal absently as he gazed outward, lost in thought. The world was still and quiet but for the faint background noise of running environmental systems and the humming of the lighting.

Connelly sat on the edge of the bed in his sleeping quarters. The lights were off, the only light coming from the hallway through the slightly open doorway. He was dressed for a hike. He rubbed his face with both hands.

He stood then, reached down and picked up his backpack.

He worked his way through the halls and then across the control room to the panel to the access shaft. He pressed his palm on the ident panel and the door slid aside with a soft whoosh.

The day was just dawning, the sunrise spreading light and color across the landscape and the clearing. Connelly took hold of his hiking staff and moved away from the access obelisk as the door closed behind him. He stepped over to the bench, set the backpack down and rested the staff against the bench.

He sat, watched the sunrise.

"Box... so what did you find out?" He closed his eyes to the warmth of the sun. "What the hell's going on?"

"I am afraid the information is rather unsettling," said Box. The device was tucked into Connelly's shirt pocket.

"You not telling me what's happening is what's unsettling."

"Of course. However, I do not believe this is going to clear things up for you."

"Box..."

"Yes, sir," said Box. A moment's hesitation, and then, "Point Zero no longer exists."

Connelly opened his eyes, stared ahead at the horizon. "Excuse me, what?"

"Yes. It seems there was an incident. The Major was of the belief that it was something that occurred between 100K and 95K that resulted in the loss of Point Zero."

"What incident? What happened? Something we did? A Monitor?"

"The Major did not know," said Box. "But he believed that it occurred at some point in the timeline between 100K and now."

"What, so we're trapped here?"

"Until whatever was done can be undone."

"Bloody great." Connelly leaned forward, rested his elbows on his knees and clasped his hands. "And just how do we do that?"

"Such was the goal of the new mission as it was defined by the Major. He placed a Monitor every 1,000 years going back to the original 100,000 year mark. With the six of you in position, he was going to place himself into stasis with plans to come out at the time of Point Zero."

Connelly finished thinking through that line of reasoning. "And so then study the data crystals from all the Monitors, determine what happened that changed everything, and set things right again. And all is well."

"In so many words."

"Something went wrong?"

"I do not know," said Box. "I do not know that all the Monitors were successfully placed, I do not know that the Major successfully placed himself in stasis, and if he did, whether he in fact revived at Point Zero. Consider... if Point Zero does not exist, what exactly would he have awakened to?

Connell thought on that comment as he watched the sun complete its rise from the horizon.

"Right," he said. "Okay, so... and this version of the Major? The A-I that he created?"

"I found nothing specifically relating to the A-I. We can assume that it was created to oversee the Monitors while the Major was unavailable."

"And this A-I... he, uh, he hasn't gone like, evil A-I on us, has he? After all these millennia? Out now to destroy humanity as payback for all the bad we've done?"

"No. I don't think so."

"Right." Connelly straightened and looked about them. It was full daylight. He stood up, reached down and picked up his backpack. "We'll see, I suppose."

"Yes sir," Box stated.

"A lot of questions still need answering. Most of 'em, as a matter of fact."

"Many of them may be answered once we reach the circle of stones."

"Such as what happened to the Major."

"Perhaps," said Box.

Connelly didn't respond to that. He reached down and picked up his hiking staff.

"We're not going directly there, are we?" asked Box. It was more of an observation than a question.

"No. We're not. First, I want to get a look at another of the outposts." He half turned and gave a nod, indicating direction. "The nearest one is that way, no more than half a day."

"What answers do you seek at an outpost abandoned thousands of years ago?"

Connelly started forward. "We shall see what we see, dear Box."

Six

Connelly turned off the main trail and followed this much narrower, meandering trail for almost an hour, followed it eventually into a side valley offshoot from the main Alpha Valley.

This smaller valley was thick with lush vegetation and crisscrossed with numerous narrow animal trails. Connelly frequently had to push through tall brush, his clothes quickly soaked from the heavy, broad damp leaves. On those occasions when he stepped out into open clearings, he often stopped to wring out his wet shirt and would spend a few minutes in the sun.

Several hours in, he entered another clearing, this one wide and open. He slipped out of his backpack, set his staff down and pulled out his canteen.

"Time, Box?"

"Two hours, twelve minutes since entering this valley."

Connelly took a second swallow, then a third. He closed the canteen.

"Good, good… we must be getting close." He looked up to the sky, spoke as he again started forward. "You know, Box, my life would be a lot easier if you had GPS."

"That would require satellites. What you ask for is—"

"I know that, Box," said Connelly, cutting him off. "You know I know that. I think you just like poking me with a stick; it gives your circuits a rush."

"Lieutenant…"

"I swear, you're more human every day."

Twenty minutes later he stepped out of the trailhead and into a long, narrow clearing. He slowed, looked about as he took a few more steps.

A thick bramble stood against a short, steep hillside. He moved toward it, used his staff to push aside the vines.

He saw only darkness within.

He lifted the staff and struck the end of it against a solid surface within the brush. The sound was dull, hollow.

He pushed his way forward, ignoring the thorny vines. Finding the smooth surface, Connelly reached out and pushed. There was a moment of resistance and then the door collapsed inward and fell to the ground.

Stepping over the fallen door, Connelly found himself in the ruins of Outpost Four. The ceiling had collapsed, and daylight was coming through and into what remained of the interior. Studying the debris, he saw little that was recognizable. Wood was long gone. Metal and some plastic remained.

"The outpost, all right," he said.

"I doubt there is much remaining," Box stated.

"You're right about that."

The layout of the outpost was the same as Connelly's Outpost Six. He worked his way toward the far corner.

"Lieutenant Connelly, what do you expect to find?" asked Box.

"We shall see what we shall see."

"How could you—"

"It's an expression, Box. How long have we been together?" He reached the far corner. "Don't answer that."

"I had not intended to," Box stated, rather defensively.

Connelly pushed aside thick ivy. He found an opening and stepped through and into a tiny back room.

Here too the ceiling had collapsed. Connelly lifted aside rubble strewn across the floor. He found the remains of a small compartment set in the floor. Within, he found what should have been a sealed container. It appeared to be damaged.

"Yep," he sighed. He didn't sound all that pleased. He sat back on his heels. "There it is."

"Lieutenant?"

"The time capsule."

"And the data crystal?"

"The time capsule was broken into," said Connelly. "The data crystal is destroyed."

"How can that be?"

"Intentional. The question is, who did it?"

"I see."

Connelly stood up and worked his way back to the main room of the outpost.

"Someone didn't want the information reaching Point Zero," he said, picking his way carefully through the debris.

"That supposes the person who destroyed the data crystal understood its purpose," said Box.

"That it does."

"Lieutenant... you were expecting this?"

"I suspected it. It makes sense, considering." Connelly stepped out of the ruin and into the open clearing. "And so... we are alone here. There will be nothing from Point Zero."

"There is no Point Zero."

"Or if there is, either they never heard from us or what they did hear from us was bad."

"But your data crystal. From Outpost Six. It remains intact."

For the moment... thought Connelly.

"To the circle of stones, then," he said.

Seven

Connelly knelt beside his backpack and brought out a light jacket, slipped into it then as he stepped across the campsite and settled in before the small campfire. He picked up the stick that was on the ground beside him and absently poked at the flames. The open valley was visible beyond the campsite, the whole world graying with the dusk and the coming night.

The night passed quietly, and he managed to get a few hours sleep. He started out again after a light breakfast just past dawn. He continued to follow the main trail up the center of the valley until he came to a well-defined junction where the main trail continued straight ahead and a slightly narrower path veered left.

He took the left fork, followed the trail as it wound through increasingly thick, tall brush. After an hour's travel he noticed the terrain starting to rise. The path took him into a wide, gently sloping bowl and then gradually upslope.

He rounded a bend in the trail, came face to face with three Alphas. He quickly noted more were half-hidden in the brush.

A very, very quiet bunch...

One of the Alphas stepped forward one step nearer Connelly. It grunted, jerked its head up and forward. It looked into the brush to either side.

A number of faces looked back at him. They grunted out encouragingly to their companion.

It looked back to Connelly. It wore a thin smile.

Well, that's new. And a bit unnerving...

Connelly nonetheless smiled in return. He held the smile as he spoke calmly to Box.

"Well, Box. It appears we are to be the guests of one of the Alpha tribes.

Box said nothing. The A-I knew when to keep silent.

Connelly held his staff out to the Alpha in a surrendering gesture.

The Alpha grinned openly as he reached out and took the staff. It grunted loudly to the others of the tribe, then lifted his free hand up in a half wave, signaling the group to move out.

They formed a line and started ahead, Connelly in the midst of the line.

"At least they're taking us in the right direction," he said.

The Alpha walking behind him gave Connelly a shove and growled crossly at him. Connelly stumbled forward, regained his footing and continued. He looked briefly back at the Alpha, gave a slight smile and quickly focused ahead.

"Quite the touchy bunch."

There was another shove from behind.

Connelly had noted throughout his earlier observations of the Alphas that they were generally affable and quite social and seldom in any particular hurry. Such was the case over the next several hours. They kept a steady pace, but were in no rush. They were often jovial with one another, joking and chuckling and occasionally rough with one another.

Connelly, however, was to keep his mouth shut and keep moving. The Alpha following directly behind him was quick to give him a shove and disapproving growl whenever Connelly spoke up or turned a glance one way or the other. So he quickly fell in line and fell silent.

After about two hours they arrived at a well-used clearing along the main river in the valley. Connelly was pushed to the ground in front of a thick bush. Several Alphas sat across the clearing from him as the others went to the riverbank.

It was midday, the sun was high overhead and warm.

Two of those at the riverbank rose up and returned to the clearing. They stood in front of Connelly, stared down at him. They each had a curious look, as if they knew something he didn't and...

The one with the staff poked at Connelly.

They both let out primitive guttural laughs.

The other then reached down and poked a finger at Connelly's side, grasped at Connelly's flesh. He straightened then and held onto his own belly as if testing for plumpness.

They both made light, cheerful yum-yum noises, laughed again, shoving playfully at each other before moving away to join the others on the other side of the clearing.

Connelly spoke matter-of-factly to Box.

"I can't say as I'm totally comfortable with that," he said.

"If I am interpreting correctly, then I would agree that should the situation play out unchecked, it would not be good for you."

"Hey... I go down, you're going down with me."

One of the Alphas gave him a threatening eye.

"Apparently food is supposed to be silent," Connelly mumbled, He attempted a pleasant smile in the Alpha's direction. "Hello," he said.

The Alpha let out a long, low rumbling growl.

Connelly tried to speak to Box then without moving his lips.

"Alphas... not quite the conversationalists as the Littles."

One of the other Alphas stood and took a step nearer Connelly, offered a menacing glare. Connelly smiled apologetically, tried to speak to Box without moving his lips.

"Though perhaps equally as short-tempered."

He fell silent, and a few minutes later they were on the move again.

Several hours later, Connelly was led into a well-defined campsite clearing, hard ground with patches of scrubby grass, large stones positioned to use as seats. At the far side stood an eight foot tall stake with rawhide ties hanging from near the top. Beyond the stake was an open field of grassland and low shrubs.

Connelly was led over to the stake. He struggled as he was tied by the wrists overhead. Those doing the securing appeared to be amused by the situation. They were grinning broadly and offering one another primitive chuckles.

Several were dancing lightly about the clearing.

"Okay, fellas, this really isn't funny anymore," he said. "Come on. Cut me loose, or I might just get angry. And I am not the best of party guests when I'm upset."

The members of the Alpha tribe ignored Connelly's jabbering. They finished their work, moved back, stood in a half-circle several yards from their prisoner.

They took a moment to admire their work.

At one word from one of the tribe, they all turned in tandem and quietly left the clearing.

"Was it something I said?" asked Connelly. "I did warn you, you know."

He was alone.

He looked about, sizing up his situation. He struggled at his ties, then relaxed as best he could.

He put on a dark frown.

"Oh, boy."

Connelly was half-asleep, which was the best he could do being tied to the stake, bound at the wrists above his head. His eyes were closed, his chin resting on his chest.

The faint sound of scuffling and rustling came from somewhere outside the clearing.

Connelly lifted his head and opened his eyes.

Eight of the Littles entered the clearing behind Connelly. Two were carrying overstuffed bags, a third carried a tall stool.

The bags were left on the ground in the center of the clearing. The Little creature with the stool positioned it behind the stake that Connelly was tied to.

"Hey, guys," said Connelly. "I wasn't expecting to see you folks again so soon."

The Little creatures said nothing. They freed Connelly from the stake, leaving his hands bound. Connelly spoke quietly to Box as he smiled at first to one Little, then another.

"Box, for now let's keep your presence between you and me," he said. "It would appear the Alphas have sold me to the Littles. I'm downright popular."

He spoke then directly to the Littles.

"I hope you don't take what happened at our previous get-together personally," he said.

The Littles continued to ignore Connelly's rambling. They directed him back the way they had come, leading him from the clearing and across the grassy field.

Eight

The Littles led Connelly across an open field and toward the two hundred foot tall wall of trees. Entering the Black Forest, he found himself once again travelling across the permanent dark twilight of the forest floor. Without the use of his flashlight, he couldn't really see where he was going, other than between and around the darker shapes that were the great trees and twenty-foot high ferns.

The Littles appeared able to see in the near darkness just fine. At least, they clearly knew where they were going. And other than an occasional hushed comment, they seldom spoke. Connelly was again struck by how quiet the Black Forest was. It was a silent world.

They followed a winding, twisting trail for what must have been two or three hours, then the group entered the village of the Littles. Connelly was led into the center of the small community. Around them were dozens of lightly-framed structures, if not actual buildings. Littles were moving in and out of the smaller surrounding trees, others scrambled up the trunks of the nearer giant trees, all with an eye to the human that was being brought into their midst.

Connelly was taken to a post and bound to a ring attached two feet above the ground. The Littles stepped away.

Standing beside the post, he looked down at the bindings; securely tied. He looked up then, just caught sight of the last of the Littles disappearing into the dark. He glanced casually again around the clearing; the structures, the lamps; another quick glance down at his bindings.

"I think we may have underestimated our friends, Box."

Box said nothing. Connelly again studied their surroundings.

"We appear to be alone, at least for the moment," he stated quietly.

"And your circumstances?" asked Box.

"They may be holding our earlier meeting against me." Another glance around the village. "Littles village. Full-on structures on the ground. Stairs leading into the canopy of trees along the perimeter. All in all, socially, culturally, they are way ahead of the Alphas."

"We suspected as much, Lieutenant."

"They're pretty good at knots, too." Connelly struggled at his bindings. "What is it with the locals and putting humans to the stake?"

Box assumed this was a rhetorical question and did not respond.

Connelly slid to the ground, his back to the post. He got as comfortable as he could, considering his position, and waited.

He didn't have to wait long, what he estimated as only a few minutes. There was movement across the plaza.

Three Littles entered the village. One was a head taller than the other two, walked with strong, sure confidence, as if he was certain of his role.

"Ah," Connelly said quietly to Box. "Their leader doth approacheth."

"Be wary, Lieutenant Connelly."

"Middle name, Box."

The Village Leader stood before Connelly, the assistants stepping up beside him.

Connelly looked up at Leader. "Good evening," he said.

There was no response from Leader, no reaction from any of the Littles.

"So, you be the big Kahuna around here?" asked Connelly, putting on a faux grin.

Village Leader turned his head slightly, studied Connelly as he contemplated the question.

"The leader," Connelly tried again. "Are you the boss?"

Village Leader studied Connelly some more. He lifted a hand then, indicated the surrounding village.

"Leader," he stated precisely. "Village."

Connelly was a little taken aback at hearing Village Leader speaking the two simple English words so clearly. He cleared his throat, shifted position.

"You, uh... you speak English?"

"English?"

"English. Language. The words you speak are in English."

"Yes. English." Village Leader thought on that for a moment. "We... watch."

"Watch," said Connelly. He grumbled then to himself, to Box, "I thought that was my job."

Village Leader's expression betrayed no emotion. Connelly tried to put on a smile, in spite of his current physical circumstances. His words, however, took on a bit of a snarky tone.

"You speak it very well. English. Great watching. Really." He indicated his bindings. "So what's the deal here?"

Village leader lifted his head while continuing to look down on Connelly. He firmly set his jaw.

"Stone," he stated flatly.

"Excuse me?"

Village Leader turned his gaze to somewhere beyond the village. He lifted hand, pointed outward.

"High Leader," he said. He continued to look outward. After a few moments he nodded, as if to some inner thought. He wore a slight smile.

Connelly frowned.

"Right," he said. "So, you're not the big Kahuna, then."

§

Connelly lay asleep, sitting on the ground with his back against the post. About him, several Littles milled about the village, the world eerily quiet.

He woke, shifted about and straightened as best he could with his hands bound to the post ring. He looked calmly about, noted where the Littles were. He spoke to Box under his breath.

"Box... was I out long?"

"One hour, forty minutes," Box said quietly.

"Did I miss anything?"

"I have been hearing comings and goings over the last few minutes."

"Quiet bunch, aren't they?" Connelly continued to study his surroundings, the Littles moving silently about the village. "No sign of Little Kahuna."

"I have not heard the Village Leader's voice."

One of the Littles approached then, stood a few feet in front of Connelly. He looked curiously at Connelly, cocked his head slightly to one side and studied the human.

Connelly forced a grin, nodded his head in greeting.

"Hey," he said. "How are ya?"

The Little said nothing. He straightened his head as another Little approached and stood beside him. Several more Littles came up behind Connelly; one began untying his bindings from the post ring. As he did, more Littles began gathering, encircling Connelly, cautiously looking on.

Village Leader moved through the group and stood directly in front of Connelly. He lifted his hand up, indicating Connelly should stand.

"Ah. Gotcha," said Connelly. He grumbled as he rolled onto his knees and stood. "You people need to make up your minds."

The group slowed as they approached a narrow creek. The Littles ahead of Connelly moved forward and spread out. They knelt at the bank and drank. Those behind Connelly moved to the left and right, stood watch. When the first group finished drinking, Village Leader stepped up beside Connelly, urged him forward to the creek. Connelly nodded without speaking, approached the bank and knelt down. The other Littles moved up to the creek as well, to Connelly's left and right, as the first group stepped across the narrow brook and waited on the opposite bank.

Connelly cupped his hands and drank. The water was a little warm, but it didn't taste bad at all. Still, he would have preferred his canteen and a purification tablet.

After a long march beyond the creek, Connelly began to notice a change in the dark up ahead. There was a flat blackness, a wall of darkness in the distance. It stood in the twilight thirty feet high.

The group approached a wall of woven sticks, canes and stalks. The line of Littles, with Connelly walking in the middle, marched single-file through a narrow opening in the wall. Connelly was led into the heart of a large, enclosed plaza. Lanterns were hung on the wall of woven sticks, putting the entire clearing into a golden glow.

A female Little sat on primitive throne positioned at the far end of the plaza. The High Leader was no larger than any other Little, but she had an air of authority about her manner. Her garment was more colorful than the clothing of the other Littles, and she wore a modest crown of wood and leaf and twig.

Three attendant Littles stood formally in a line to the High Leader's right.

She waved a hand for Connelly to be brought nearer. Village Leader took hold of Connelly's arm, and without a word guided him forward until they were standing two paces from the throne.

Village Leader stepped back and away. His work was apparently done.

High Leader looked unemotionally down upon the human. When she finally spoke, the words were in broken English.

"I see you, Monitor."

"Right," sighed Connelly. "I uh, see you too."

Another Little leader speaking in English...

He mumbled then to Box. "You heard that, right?"

"I heard."

High Leader straightened.

"I am High Leader." She waved a hand about her, indicating all the Littles. "We wait. Thousand cycles. I welcome Monitor." She lifted a hand from one arm of the throne, held it out and indicated Connelly. "Our Monitor."

"Um... thank you," said Connelly, a bit uncomfortably.

"Next stone."

Again with the stone...

"Stone? I, uh..." Connelly fumbled in his thoughts, mumbled to Box, "Does she mean...?"

"The circle of stones," said Box.

Connelly frowned. "It sounds way more ominous the way she says it." Connelly cleared his throat, smiled nervously at High Leader. "Stone? Next stone?"

High Leader stood. "Next stone waits. We go."

There was immediate movement all about the large throne clearing as the Littles all set about to prepare to leave.

Again? What is it with you people?

High Leader stepped down, took a step nearer to Connelly. She remained stoic, displayed no emotion.

The three attendant Littles stepped forward with their leader. She glanced briefly in their direction. As if on signal, they turned and started toward the trailhead at the perimeter of the clearing. High Leader followed. Other Littles moved in behind Connelly, two more to either side of him.

They waited expectantly.

Connelly gave a thin smile to one, then the other.

"Sure. I was, you know, headin' that way anyway."

They gave Connelly a stern look. Up ahead, the three attendant Littles and High Leader had already reached the trailhead.

"Right," sighed Connelly. "We go..."

Nine

Connelly and his companions traveled the forest floor in a long line, moving in and out of hazy streaks of light that reached down from the canopy. The edge of the forest was less than an hour from the throne clearing, and it was still midday when they left the forest and came out of the trees and into the outer edges of Alpha Valley.

They worked their way to the main trail and followed it up the valley. There was very little talk, and when Connelly on occasion looked back to the Little walking behind him and would offer a smile, the Little would return a stern gaze.

They left the main trail at a wide but rather obscure trailhead and within minutes were following a steep trail up the side of a hillside of dry grass and short, scrubby brush. At times Connelly found himself taking hold of exposed rock as he pulled himself up.

"Aren't we there yet?" Connelly grumbled.

"It would be difficult for me to extrapolate our current location in relation to the circle of stones," said Box.

"You stay out of this."

Connelly looked up at High Leader as she looked down at him. She said nothing.

Connelly gave another half-smile. "Coming, dear."

High Leader frowned as she turned about and continued up the hillside.

"The lady needs a sense of humor."

They continued the rest of the way in silence, reaching a trail that ran under the ridge. They followed this horizontal trail around the ridge and out onto a large landing. It was set just below the ridge, forming a jutting ledge that looked out across the great valley below. The ground was smooth, with tufts of grass and weed here and there.

About the perimeter of the clearing were a number of granite rock formations towering ten to twelve feet high. Standing atop these rocks were a number of Littles.

In the center of the clearing was an array of seven closed rectangular stone boxes set in a circular pattern, as the spokes of a wheel, the head of each stone box facing inward to the heart of the circle.

Connelly was led onto the landing, the Littles coming in behind him and moving out along the perimeter of the clearing. Connelly followed High Leader into the heart of the circle of stones.

"Coffins," whispered Connelly.

"Lieutenant?" asked Box.

"The circle of stones. They look like coffins. You know what a sarcophagus is?"

"I do."

High Leader moved to one side with her entourage of three as Connelly moved to the very center of the clearing. He turned slowly about, studying the stone boxes.

"Seven of 'em," he said.

"One for each Monitor, and –"

"One for the Major," Connelly finished. He gave High Leader a nervous smile. "So, what's the plan, High Leader? Singing 'round the campfire? Marshmallows? Hot dogs?" A glance to the boxes. "Mummification?"

High Leader said nothing.

So, that would be no, then...

She rested the palm of one hand against her chest. There was a light chattering about the clearing, the Littles about the clearing moving slow, almost reverential. Those on the ground moved closer into the center of the clearing, closing in about the coffin-like stone boxes.

High Leader's entourage stepped back, leaving their leader and Connelly standing alone within the heart of the circle of stones.

High Leader was expressionless. She cocked her head slightly to one side. She calmly lifted one hand and raised a finger. As she did, the Littles about them fell silent. Those standing on the ground went to one knee, while those on the surrounding rocks stood unmoving.

High Leader waited, let the enveloping silence grow heavy.

She straightened then, spoke then to her people. Her voice was soft, her tone melodic.

Theh nemoh la deh. Mehloh nahm. Toh theh lohn noh.

The kneeling Littles rose and remained silent. The Littles standing atop the tall rock formations responded in unison to the High Leader.

Theh mehneh lohn noh.

The clearing again grew heavily quiet. Three of the Littles standing along the perimeter of the circle moved aside, allowing another Little to step into the circle. He approached Connelly and High Leader, walking slowly, carrying a metallic canister with all the deference due a ritualistic artifact.

Connelly whispered to Box. "Their ritual artifact is a sealed canister."

The approaching Little gave Connelly a brief, harsh glare as he passed, not appreciating the apparent disrespect for the ceremony in progress. Connelly responded with an apologetic grin.

The Little and High Leader stood facing one another for several moments.

High Leader held out her hands.

Tah meh shah toh. Ehm nah doh.

At that, the other Little lifted the canister, placed it gently into High Leader's waiting hands. He took several steps back then until he was standing directly beside Connelly.

He dropped to one knee, looked expectantly up to Connelly.

Connelly looked from High Leader to the kneeling Little, back to High Leader. She appeared to also be waiting for something.

Connelly gradually realized what she was waiting for. He also then dropped to one knee, beside the kneeling Little.

High Leader gave silent acknowledgment, then stepped over to one of the stones. She placed the canister on the lid, slid aside a small panel set into the side of the canister, and pressed a hidden keypad.

"She knows how to open the canister," Connelly mumbled.

"Interesting," Box answered.

The Little kneeling beside Connelly turned another irritated gaze to the human.

Sorry...

High Leader opened the canister. All the Littles in the clearing intoned a brief, melodic chant.

Theh moh loh. Theh mohn lah.

The clearing again fell silent. High Leader lifted a small, square device from inside the canister; metal and plastic, about three inches square.

She lifted the device above her head. *Theh lohn Mehloh deh.*

The Littles in the clearing respond in chant: *Mehneh lohn noh deh. Mehol theh.*

High Leader lowered the device. She moved to the head of the stone box, carefully set the device into position on the stone lid.

She noheh deh noh.

Mehloh theh noh, responded the Littles.

There was a gritty sound as the lid began to slide open, back from the head of the container.

Opening the coffin...

"Uh, oh," mumbled Connelly.

"Lieutenant?" prompted Box.

"I'll, uh... tell you later." *Assuming I, uh...*

The lid slid back a third the length of the stone and stopped. High Leader moved to the side, reached in and lifted another canister from within the stone box.

The Littles intoned another chant. *Mehloh noh. Mehloh theh noh.*

High Leader turned and stepped toward Connelly, who was still on one knee. She held the canister out to him. Connelly hesitated, finally reached out and took the canister.

High Leader spoke as if part of the ritual, the words clumsy yet clearly in English.

"We the people... future," she stated. "Major... lift the people. Major... make future so."

The circle of stones clearing again went quiet. Connelly had no idea what he was expected to do. He hesitated. He looked from the canister to High Leader, back to the canister. He gave a quick glance to the open stone box, then.

So, then I'm not going to, uh...

High Leader took a step back, looked about at the Littles standing in the enclosing circle, then to those on the tall rock formations along the clearing perimeter.

Loh theh noh shah toh. Ah Leh, she said.

And with that the Littles standing in the engulfing circle silently began to back away. They turned and filed away the way they came. The Littles standing atop the rock formations backed away, disappeared from view.

Within moments there was only High Leader and Connelly.

Connelly weighed the canister resting in his hands. "This is... this is from the Major?" he asked.

"It is."

"Ya' got any idea what's in here?" Connelly continued to study the sealed canister.

High Leader's expression was solemn. "My task... complete," she stated.

"Right. Right," said Connelly. "Long time coming, eh?"

High Leader considered the meaning of the question. She gave the hint of a nod, pursed her lips.

"My life," she said. "My ancestors before me. Many ancestors."

"Oh, I get that."

High Leader turned back to the open stone box. She pressed the device that was still sitting on the lid. The lid slid closed with a hollow grinding noise.

At the sight of the box closing, Connelly mumbled "So glad to see that. Smiling here."

"Lieutenant?" asked Box.

"Tell ya' later."

High Leader picked up the device, stepped back to Connelly.

"For you," she said.

Connelly tucked the canister that he was holding under his arm and took the device.

"And this is for...?"

"Answers come to you when answers you need."

Connelly stared down at the device in his hand as High Leader stepped past him and left the clearing of the circle of stones.

Alone...

"Right."

Ten

Connelly was sitting on the stone bench a dozen paces from the Central access obelisk. Sunset was a few minutes away, he watched as the sun slowly descended toward the horizon.

He wondered now about the bench. It hadn't been here when he first arrived from Point Zero, had assumed until recently that the Major had placed it here. It would have taken work, dragging it from wherever the stone had come.

Now, knowing that the other Monitors had lived out their lives in the five millennia before him, he realized it could have been any of them.

Good decision in any case. This was a favorite spot of Connelly's; and sunset was a favorite time.

Box interrupted his reverie.

"Lieutenant Connelly, in order to determine what is in the canister, you will need to look inside the canister."

The sealed canister was on the bench beside him. Box was resolute that they get on with it. They had returned from the circle of stones more than an hour earlier, and had yet to actually go into the center.

"Soon enough, Box. Soon enough. I'm just not in the mood to deal with A-I Major right now."

"Ah. And the electronic key needed to open the canister is in Central."

Both were silent for a few moments.

"I do love the sunsets here," said Connelly at last. He continued to watch the sun descend nearer and nearer the horizon. "Major set that ritual up, you know; created an elaborate ceremony for the Littles."

"Yes," stated Box.

Connelly reached over and picked up the canister. He studied it, weighed it in one hand.

"He intended that each Monitor receive one of these," he said, considering. "Can you imagine? Generation after generation, the Littles preparing for one brief moment every thousand years, just to hand off one of these?"

"By their very nature, the Littles were the perfect choice for such a task."

"I suppose that's so. They are... interesting." He returned his gaze to the setting sun, now only moments remaining. "And more than that. They worshiped the Major. I wonder how he managed that."

"I would think that he worked very hard at establishing such a relationship. Such would be vital if he wished for the ritual to continue across the millennia."

"So it was important." To himself then, "Weird."

The sun finished its descent into the horizon. Streaks of orange and yellow and red reached out across the landscape, slowly faded to gray. The world grew steadily into dusk.

Connelly stood at the island counter in Central's main control room. The open canister was on the countertop in front of him, several wires running from the opening. Connelly was wearing a headset plugged into a jack in the counter, he was listening to the small, tinny sound of the Major's voice.

"Nothing we do will prevent Point Zero from vanishing," said the Major. "As it is the very future itself that is lost. By their actions. Not ours. Nothing we do here will change that. I have tried. What remains to us is to endeavor for a new future, a future that belongs to the Littles and the Alphas."

Connelly remained at the counter, listening to the message from the distant past, from the Major. The control room was quiet but for the environmental systems running in the background and the hint of the Major's voice leaking from the headset. It continued for another several minutes.

Finished then, Connelly pulled off the headset, set it on the counter.

The relative silence in the room was broken when the voice of A-I Major came softly over the speakers.

"Have you finished listening to the Major's message, Lieutenant?"

"I have."

Silence again. Box then spoke up.

"What did the Major have to say, Lieutenant Connelly?"

Connelly turned slowly about, leaned back against the counter and folded his arms across his chest. His expression was hesitant.

"The Major wasn't trying to make things right in order to get us all back to Point Zero," he said. "He's stopping us from getting to Point Zero in order to make things right."

"Lieutenant," said Box. "We suspected as much. Did we not?"

"Something like that. I suppose. Sort of."

A-I Major interrupted. "Can you explain, please?"

Connelly rose up out of his thoughts. "The future, it would seem, belongs to the Alphas and the Littles."

"But the Littles and Alphas are both dead ends," stated Box. "The valley and the Black Forest are—"

"Apparently our continued presence here can change that," said Connelly, cutting him off. "Can change everything. The Major believed it to be so. So much so that he has ensured that no one can return to Point Zero."

"I see," said Box.

"And not just the Monitors. He was also rather emphatic that none of our data reach Point Zero."

"That would explain the condition of the data crystal that we found at Outpost Four."

"I am directed to destroy my data crystal," said Connelly. "The same order was given to all the Monitors."

A-I Major interrupted again. "I hesitate to bring this up, due perhaps to the Major's role in my creation, but... was the Major insane?"

"He saw something," said Connelly, slowly shaking his head no. He began disconnecting the wiring and the headset from the canister. "Maybe when he returned to Point Zero, to what happened, he saw something. Something really bad. Something that eventually led him to believe that the world must be taken in a new direction."

"I understand," said Box. "Why couldn't this message be kept at Central and delivered to the Monitors through standard channels? Why this elaborate ritual with the Littles."

"Me," said A-I Major with some certainty. "It was me. Major was concerned how I might respond to this."

"That may have had something to do with it." Connelly sounded doubtful. "But I'm thinking it had more to do with the Littles. I think it may have been part of setting them on a path that he wanted them to follow."

"And perhaps you and the other Monitors onto paths of your own," said Box.

"Perhaps." Connelly started across the room toward the hallway. "At the moment, my path leads to the shower, the mess, and to bed. In that order."

Connelly was sitting on the hilltop ridge, binoculars in hand, looking out across the narrow valley below. His hiking staff and backpack were in the grass beside him, Box sitting on the backpack.

A group of Alphas were milling about a small encampment on the valley floor.

Connelly lowered the binoculars, continued to look down into the valley.

"The Alphas and the Littles were evolutionary dead ends." His tone was conversational. He glanced once at the device sitting on the backpack, turned his attention back to the encampment below.

"As I have stated," said Box.

"This valley and everything in it was an aberration."

"One of the primary reasons for the original mission in which you and the other Monitors were to participate."

"Yeah," sighed Connelly. "So you say."

"Such was the mission description."

"Right." Connelly lifted the binoculars and returned to studying the group of Alphas. "I was there."

"Of course."

Connelly frowned as he again lowered the binoculars. "The others. The other Monitors. What did they do when faced with... this?"

"They destroyed their data crystals."

"But how did they live out their lives? What did they do? How did their presence here impact our friends down there?"

"We see the Littles and the Alphas as they are now, Lieutenant. Without the other data crystals, we know nothing of what they were like previously beyond what little data we were given in the mission briefings."

"Did any of it really change things at Point Zero?" Connelly wondered aloud. "Does that world of 2058 now belong to the Littles? The Alphas?"

Box did not respond. He had no answer to those questions, and he knew that Connelly knew that.

"I am not smiling here, Box," said Connelly.

He let out a tired, frustrated sigh. He let the seconds pass, then got slowly to his feet. He took a step down the hill, glanced down into the valley again.

"We don't know that," he said.

"Lieutenant?"

Connelly looked back at the Box device set atop his backpack, spoke directly at it.

"We don't know that all the Monitors destroyed their data crystals. We know only that Monitor Four destroyed his."

"That is so," said Box. "And if they didn't?"

"Then, despite the Major's orders, Point Zero will have received info from the past." He stepped back toward his gear. He looked down at Box. "But if Point Zero no longer exists, it doesn't matter. Does it?"

"Unless the data crystals not being destroyed is the reason that Point Zero no longer exists. Such was Major's concern."

Connelly picked up Box and stuffed the A-I device into his jacket pocket.

"My brain hurts." He started walking along the ridge.

"We're going to visit all the outposts. Aren't we?" asked Box.

"Yup."

"And you were planning this all along, weren't you?"

"Yup."

Eleven

The night beyond the circle of light from the small campfire was near black, the flickering firelight reflecting on Connelly's face and the ruin of the outpost behind him.

This was his third outpost in a week. Each had been pretty much the same. He had dug through piles of metal and plastic covered in millennia of vegetation, getting to his hands and knees to reach in through the rubble, looking for the floor compartment and the canister containing the data capsule.

To be disappointed each time.

There was one outpost yet to go.

He reached down and picked up a stick, absently poked at the fire. Sparks rose up into the night.

Connelly scrambled down a steep, overgrown trail and stepped out into the middle of a wide clearing.

The ground was clear of debris, as if recently swept clean. There was a primitive sculpture of sticks and twine and bamboo in the heart of the clearing. It faintly resembled a humanoid figure.

"Things do be getting curiouser," said Connelly.

"Yes?" prompted Box.

Connelly was looking warily into the shadows and brush just beyond the clearing. There was an open trailhead to the left, and a gurgling creek was visible further downslope.

"The locals appear to have an emotional attachment to Outpost Five."

"In what way, Lieutenant?"

"Housekeeping, for one," said Connelly brushing at the swept and manicured ground with his feet. He approached the sculpture. "And primitive arts and crafts."

"I see," said Box, noncommittally. "And have you found the outpost?"

Connelly moved to the back of the clearing, where the level ground met the steep terrain that he had scrambled down moments earlier.

"I'm looking now." He pushed aside thick vines and bramble. Hidden in the vegetation was a metal door. "The door is still standing."

He reached in and pushed a palm against the metal. The door gave way and fell inward.

"Check that," he said. He leaned his staff against the wall of vegetation next to the opening and stepped into the darkness.

The roof of the outpost was still up, and the walls were still standing. Connelly brought out his flashlight. Much of the interior was in ruin. After a thousand years, only metal and plastic maintained any recognizable form.

Connelly worked his way across the room and toward the opening in the far corner.

The floor of the small back room was covered in layers of decomposed wood and twisted plastic and metal. Connelly stepped through the debris to get to the far wall. He went to his knees and pushed aside the rubble. He lifted an access in the floor and looked into the compartment beneath.

"The data container is still here," he said.

"And the data crystal?" asked Box.

"What say we find out?" Connelly reached into the compartment and brought out the container. "The container is sealed."

He stood and worked his way out of the back room, then across the main room. He stepped out of the outpost and into the clearing, the sealed container under his arm.

He stopped in mid-step.

"Uh, oh."

"Lieutenant?" asked Box.

"We have company."

There were three Alphas in the clearing. One was standing at the trailhead, the other two in the heart of the clearing near the handcrafted sculpture. Each had a wooden staff in hand. Their expressions betrayed no emotion, but none appeared aggressive at the moment.

They silently study Connelly.

Connelly struggled with a slight grin. "Good afternoon, gentlemen."

There was no response from the Alphas.

Connelly maintained his friendly expression as he spoke calmly to Box.

"I don't recognize them. I think they're from the North tribe."

"The North tribe seldom interacts with the others," said Box.

"Well, best I can figure, this is their territory."

Connelly looked from one to another of the Alphas, gave an acknowledging nod to the nearest of them.

"How are you today?" he asked. He gave the container that was tucked under his arm a pat. "I hope you don't mind." A frown and a mumble then, "I really, really hope you don't mind."

One of the Alphas frowned curiously as he looked at the object that Connelly was holding. He focused again on Connelly's face. The frown faded.

Connelly indicated the trailhead, currently blocked by one of the Alphas.

"I um... I really should be going now." He put on a weak smile. "But it's been really great talking with you."

He took a step to his left, in the general direction of the trailhead. When none of the Alphas moved, neither to stand in his way nor get out of his way, he stopped, pointed again to the trailhead.

"I go now?" he asked.

One of the Alphas growled low, grunting.

"Um, is that a yes?"

Silence.

Box's voice then, soft and calming.

"Beware your level of smart-ass, Lieutenant Connelly," he said. "They may not understand the words, but the attitude comes across loud and clear."

The Alpha standing nearest Connelly let out a low *humph* sound. It scrunched its face, relaxed it then.

It spoke a word then in English, half in a growl.

"Jack-son." It looked to the sculpture of branch and twine and bamboo. It pointed to it as it looked sharply at Connelly. "Jack-son," it repeated.

"Holy crap," said Connelly, under his breath.

"I assume that was an Alpha who spoke," said Box.

"It wasn't me."

"Rather gruff perhaps, but it was quite understandable."

"That's impossible."

The Alpha standing beside the first now spoke up. "Jack-son."

Connelly looked to the one, then other, mumbled then to Box as he wore his least threatening facial expression.

"Setting aside for a moment the fact that these are Alphas, she's been gone a thousand years."

"Her name has been passed down through the generations."

"Again... *Alphas*," stated Connelly.

"Nonetheless."

"Right. And, it would seem that she made as much an impression on them as the Major made on the Littles."

"Yes," said Box. "So it would seem."

Connelly made eye contact with each of the Alphas in turn, then rested a hand on his chest.

"I am a friend of Jackson," he said, as friendly as he could manage. "Jackson, friend."

The Alphas warily study Connelly.

"I doubt they understand, Lieutenant," said Box.

At the very least, they had heard Connelly say Jackson. But then, for all he knew, an outsider speaking her name could be a bad thing. A very, very bad thing.

"Friend," said the first Alpha. "Jack-son."

He didn't look upset.

"Yes," said Connelly. "Jackson, friend."

In your face, Box...

"Jackson, friend," repeated the Alpha.

"Right. Exactly. You... friend?"

"Friend."

The Alpha had yet to change expression. All the Alphas had the same, unsettlingly emotionless expression.

So where were they going with this back and forth friend stuff?

"Friends. All friends here," he grumbled. To himself then, "This friend really needs to leave."

He gave a slightly uncomfortable nod and smile to the nearest Alpha, took a step toward the trailhead. He hesitated then, pointed back to his hiking staff, which he had left leaning against the vegetation beside the outpost opening.

"I, uh... my..." He pointed awkwardly, side-stepped back to the staff and took hold of it. "My... staff."

He slip-slid walked across the clearing and to the trailhead. He gave the Alpha standing there a final, awkward nod.

"I'll just be... going now."

Twelve

Connelly finished dressing in clean clothes after taking a long, hot shower. He picked the container up from where he had tossed it onto his bunk. He walked a narrow hall to the main hall, turned and followed the larger hallway, the container tucked under his arm.

A-I Major had pelted him with questions about his recent outing, and hadn't been satisfied with Connelly's answers. He continued questioning him as Connelly walked the hall.

"I am not certain that I fully understand what you are saying, Lieutenant."

"What's to understand?" asked Connelly. "You know what I know. I've told you everything. You wanted me to find Major. I found him. He's in a stone box up on a mountain. Bunch of little people taking care of him."

He reached an archway on the left and stepped into the comm room. The room was small, a counter along one wall, with one chair. An equipment board was built into the wall above the counter.

A-I Major's voice followed him in.

"Your discovery in point of fact generates many more questions than it answers, Lieutenant Connelly."

Connelly settled into the chair, his response coming through in a heavy drone of a sigh.

"Man, do I hear that." He set the container on the counter. He opened it and removed the data crystal. "Why don't we see if this offers us any answers, shall we?"

He opened an access panel in the equipment board, inserted the data crystal. He flipped several switches, sat back in his chair and waited.

A female voice came through a pair of speakers set into the equipment board.

"Hey, Connelly... Jackson here. Long time, no see."

Connelly grinned. *Hey, Jackson...*

"Some weird crap going on, eh?" Jackson continued.

You got that right...

Box spoke up. "It would appear that Lieutenant Jackson has used the Outpost Five data crystal to leave a message. A message specifically intended for you."

"Ya' think?"

"Since you're listening to this," Jackson went on, "you already know that everything has gone wonkers. I can assume you've been given the line, and that you don't totally believe it."

Connelly settled back deeper into the chair...

The sun was just touching the western horizon. Sunset colors streaked across the landscape, reaching Connelly as he sat on the stone bench near the Central access obelisk.

The words of Jackson, the Monitor from Outpost Five, played back in his mind.

"So, if you're planning on trying to find a way around Major's work and get back to Point Zero, you can forget it. But not for the reason you're thinking. Ya' see, there never was a plan to return us home. Just the data. All they wanted were the data crystals."

Connelly leaned forward, elbows on his knees, clasped his hands. Jackson's words continued, not in any particular order, jumping back and forth from the message coming to him from a thousand years in the past.

"Major was part of it all, at least he knew about it. Maybe he just figured it out. I don't know what set him off, what set him against the Foundation."

"Lieutenant?" Box attempted to interrupt Connelly's thoughts. "Lieutenant?"

Connelly ignored him, perhaps didn't hear him. For the moment, there were only Jackson's words.

"I spent years in the Valley," she said. "With the Alphas. Spent more with the Littles. A most curious species, the Littles. The *First Ones*, as the Alphas call them."

Connelly stood slowly, took a step toward the setting sun.

"You take care of the Alphas," said Jackson. "The Littles call them *The Children*. They see them as the future. I didn't see it at first, but over time I..."

Connelly was still standing there, a few yards from the bench, after the sun had finished setting and the colors had begun fading to gray.

He and Box had exchanged a few words, for which Box was grateful, as grateful as an A-I could be.

He didn't want anything bad to happen to his only connection to the real world.

Connelly stuffed his hands into his jacket pockets.

"In the end, she decided not to let the data go to Point Zero," he said. "She never said why, not in so many words. It had to do with the Littles and the Alphas."

"She accepted the Major's reasoning," suggested Box.

"Maybe," said Connelly, not fully satisfied with that explanation. "Anyway, my being the only Monitor left in the timeline, I think she wanted to say hi."

"And so? What will you do, Lieutenant Connelly?"

Connelly pushed his hands deeper into his jacket pockets, took in the quickly graying dusk.

"I don't know, Box."

Connelly finished preparing his dinner at the counter and took his plate over to the middle table in the mess. He took Box from his pocket and set the device on the table beside his plate. He spoke then into the air as he stepped over to the water dispenser, his words and tone a bit hesitant.

"Hey, uh... Major. Ya' got a minute?"

"Of course, Lieutenant."

"You called all the Monitors back to Central just as you did me, right?" he asked. He finished filling the water glass and started back to the table. "I mean, when you recalled me, you said all the Monitors were being called home."

"That is correct."

Connelly sat down, set his glass on the table and pulled his plate nearer.

"So... did they hang around? Here at Central?"

There was a hesitation from A-I Major.

"Several did," he said at last. "For a time."

Connelly ate as he talked. "So, where'd they go, then?"

"I believe some returned to their outposts, at least at first. To the natives then, I would imagine. The Littles and the Alphas."

"You don't know?"

"To their outposts, initially," stated A-I Major. "Why do you ask, Lieutenant?"

Connelly looked thoughtfully up in the general direction of the disembodied voice of the A-I.

"It's just that... I gather that no one brought you news of the Major. I'm the first to do that."

"That is so."

"I take it they didn't take the news of our true situation quite as well as me, then," said Connelly. "And with you being the messenger and all..."

"I was not the messenger," A-I Major stated succinctly. In more of a conceding tone then, "However, as they realized the truth of their circumstances, I may have been the focus of their discontent."

"I can imagine." Connelly took another bite of food, glanced down to the Box device. "What about their Box devices?"

"Lieutenant?"

"Do you know what happened to the other Monitors' Boxes?"

"I do not."

There were several long moments of uncomfortable silence. Connelly inattentively poked at what was left of his meal with his fork.

"You've been alone... a really long time," he said. There was no response from A-I Major. "I mean, even if the other Monitors had stuck around, there were all those centuries in between."

"That is so."

Connelly quit pushing his food about with his fork and took another bite.

"That's gotta suck," he said.

"It has at times been unpleasant," A-I Major stated smoothly, only after a long pause. Both went silent then. Connelly continued to eat his meal, staring absently across the room.

Box did not speak at all. Connelly glanced once at the device, returned his absent gaze to the far side of the quiet room. There was only the sound of the environmental systems running in the background and the hum of the lights.

Thirteen

An early evening lay over the clearing. Horizontal shadows stretched across the circle of stones, pushed up against the tall stones along the perimeter. The last dim rays of the setting sun painted thin streaks of color across the cool, gray lids of the stone boxes.

Lieutenant Connelly entered the clearing from the only trailhead, walked into the heart of the circle of stones. He set his staff against one of the stone boxes, slipped out of his small backpack.

He glanced about the clearing as he took the access device out of a side pocket of the pack. He moved over to one of the boxes, set the device on the lid. He pressed a key on the device, straightened and stepped back.

The lid slid open to the gritty, grinding sound of stone against stone. Connelly hesitated, warily approached the open stone box. Standing stiffly, he leaned in slightly and looked inside.

The clearing was fully shrouded in deepening gray, the sun having set, the darkness coming. Connelly was sitting on one of the stone boxes. All had been opened, all were now closed.

A movement drew Connelly from his reverie. He glanced up and to one side as the High Leader of the Littles came into the clearing. He noted movement in the shadows as other Littles hovered beyond the tall rock formations along the perimeter.

High Leader came into the center of the clearing and stood in front of Connelly.

Connelly indicated the stone boxes.

"All of 'em," he said. "They're all here, then. The Monitors."

"I have been told so," said High Leader.

Connelly nodded solemnly. He spoke then as if to himself.

"They all fell in line." He indicated the box opposite. "Behind the Major."

"Major lift the people."

"Right. So you said."

"We. First Ones," said High Leader. "We... watch. We help Monitors."

"So it would seem."

"We care for the Children."

"Right." Connelly looked thoughtfully at High Leader. "The Alphas. The Children."

"We, future. Children, future."

Connelly nodded at that, returned his gaze to the circle of stones, the stone boxes.

"And so it would seem," he said.

High Leader looked outward, looked away as if she was now lost in thought. It was several moments before she returned her focus to Connelly. She indicated the device sitting on the lid beside him, then pointed to the stone box from which she had taken the canister that she had then given to Connelly.

"When you ready, Monitor, we help."

"Yeah. So I figured." Connelly stared at the box that was one day to be his sarcophagus. He leaned forward and stood up. He gathered up his backpack and his staff. "That do be a long way off, my friend. Natural causes and all that."

He picked up the device, held it out briefly before unceremoniously stuffing it into his jacket pocket. "But let's keep in touch," he said. "That good by you?"

It took High Leader a moment to sort out the meaning of the question. She then gave a short, curt nod.

"We watch Monitor," she stated.

Connelly smiled cordially, spoke affably as he started across the clearing.

"I believe this may be the start of a long and most curious friendship, Your Highness."

Fourteen

The gently sloping hills were covered in a forest of tall trees. A thick, green canopy was spread high above a sparse undergrowth on the forest floor. The figure of Connelly, little more than a silhouette, moved into and out of the shadows of the trees as he followed the winding, narrow mountain trail, his ever-present hiking staff in hand, a light backpack on his back.

He stepped into the clearing, walked past the rustic root cellar door and on toward the outpost, the wall set into the side of a brush-covered mound.

Outpost Six. His outpost.

He leaned his staff against the wall beside the door. He pressed his palm against the ident panel. There was a hard click sound. He lifted the door latch and slid it aside, opened the door.

He stepped inside his outpost, set his backpack on the table and walked across the main cabin. In the back room, he knelt down beside the compartment set into the floor and opened it. Inside was the sealed time capsule, within which resided the data crystal.

Connelly hesitated, took a long breath. He reached into the compartment then and brought out the canister. Sitting back, he weighed the canister in hand. He stood, worked his way out of the outpost.

The day was warm, the sky clear, the sun high overhead. Connelly was sitting on the riverbank, a homemade fishing pole in hand, the line in the water. His hair was longer these days, his dress more casual. A canvas bag was sitting on the ground nearby. Next to the bag was a metal thermos.

Connelly appeared quite relaxed. He glanced briefly at Box. The device was resting against a stick that Connelly had pushed into the ground, making it appear Box was kicking back and relaxing alongside Connelly.

"Another utterly uneventful day, dear Box."

There was a moment of hesitation from Box.

"You can't put it off any longer, Lieutenant," he said at last.

"Oh, sure I can," said Connelly.

"You cannot. You must destroy the data crystal. You must do so now, before something happens."

"Why?"

"Lieutenant... you should have done it a year ago. It should never have left the outpost intact."

"Why?"

"Lieutenant..."

Connelly set his pole aside, pulled the canvas bag to him, brought out a bag of ration pellets. Leaning back on one elbow, he began munching on the food.

"I wasn't ready, my friend," he said. "I'm still not ready."

"What is the purpose in delaying what must be done?" asked Box.

"I haven't decided yet." He tossed another ration pellet into his mouth. "And... I may want to leave a message. Jackson did."

"Lieutenant Jackson's message was for you. There are no Monitors to follow."

"I know that."

"Lieutenant... You do intend to wipe the current data..."

"It is what the Major wanted, isn't it?"

"He ordered you to destroy the data crystal, not just the data in the crystal."

"Same difference."

"It is not."

"Too bad." Connelly closed the bag of rations, stuffed it back into the canvas bag. He picked up the thermos, opened it and took a drink. "Hey, Box... there is something we do need to make a decision on."

He closed the thermos, set it back on the ground beside the canvas bag.

"There is the matter of you, once I'm gone."

"I have considered the options, as well," said Box.

"No doubt." said Connelly. "Me, I really see only one."

"And that would be?"

"That you join the A-I Major."

There was a long, uncomfortable pause before Box responded.

"Perhaps. When the time comes."

Connelly grinned as he reached over and picked up his fishing pole.

"Oh, so that we put off. I gotta destroy the data crystal like right now, but loading you back into Central, that can wait."

Another very long hesitation...

"I am... not ready," said Box.

Another grin from Connelly as he pulled lightly on his fishing pole.

"Uh, huh." A long pause then. "What a nice day. Eh, my friend?"

"Yes, Lieutenant," said Box. "A very nice day."

The sun was low on the horizon, sunset not far away. Connelly sat slowly and carefully on the stone bench near the Central access obelisk. His shoulder-length hair was gray, his skin pale and weathered. His eyes were clear and sharp.

The High Leader of the Littles came into the clearing. She approached Connelly, sat on the bench beside him.

"Good afternoon, Connelly."

The sun now just touched the horizon.

"Good evening, High Leader."

High Leader looked outward across the landscape. She smiled warmly.

"Yes," she said. "Evening."

The sun's rays streaked across the clearing, shone on the faces of both Connelly and High Leader. High Leader closed her eyes and wore a pleasant smile.

"Feel good."

"That it does," said Connelly.

They sat silent for several moments, took in the quiet evening.

Connelly spoke then while keeping his focus on the horizon.

"It's good to see you," he said. "Been a while."

"It has," said High Leader. "Good to see you."

They again grew silent. The sun sank below the horizon. A third of the sky was suddenly painted in dark red and deep orange.

"I do like the sunsets here." Connelly breathed out tiredly. He gave a quick glance to High Leader, returned his attention to the horizon. "Not today, my friend."

"I know," said High Leader.

Connelly managed an easy nod. He relaxed again, let out another sigh and repeated his comment of a few moments earlier.

"I do like the sunsets here."

Elderly Connelly and High Leader sat in silence then, side by side on the bench, and watched the sunset.

Two Littles stood at the edge of the central clearing, just within the brush. From here they could watch unobserved Elderly Connelly and High Leader sitting on the bench in the distance.

These Littles were dressed in future garb of slacks, shirt and flowing open robes.

They stood silent for a long time, observing the two in the distance, there expressions warm and yet somehow remote.

One then turned to the other. It gave a very slight nod. It looked back to those on the bench. As it did so, the two vanished.

High Leader felt something, sensed something. She turned slowly about and looked behind them.

She saw nothing. There was nothing.

They were alone.

She turned about again, continued to watch the sunset with her friend Connelly.

end...

www.ingramcontent.com/pod-product-compliance
Lightning Source LLC
Chambersburg PA
CBHW022048170626
46808CB00003B/1405